Herbert A. Giles

Arcana Saitica

briefly discussed in three essays on the masonic tracing boards

Herbert A. Giles

Arcana Saitica
briefly discussed in three essays on the masonic tracing boards

ISBN/EAN: 9783337399719

Printed in Europe, USA, Canada, Australia, Japan

Cover: Foto ©Andreas Hilbeck / pixelio.de

More available books at **www.hansebooks.com**

ARCANA SAITICA

BRIEFLY DISCUSSED

IN

THREE ESSAYS

ON THE

MASONIC TRACING BOARDS.

AMOY:

PRINTED BY A. A. MARÇAL,

1879.

PREFACE.

IN defence of the following short essays I will only say that my attention being drawn to the explanations given in the established lectures on Masonic tracing boards I set myself to investigate their accuracy, with what result I shall presently show.

I do not claim any originality for what I have written: it is simply the result of a considerable amount of, unhappily, somewhat desultory reading; and those who have happened to study the works of Dulaure, Dupuis, Sainte Croix, Knight, Faber, Higgins, Inman, Cory and many others treating on kindred subjects will be at no loss to discover whence I have drawn my information.

I believe that to a large number of Masons the esoteric meaning of the symbols and ceremonies in constant use and practice amongst us is either unknown or disregarded; but it surely cannot be uninteresting, even as a matter of history, to know whence they were derived, and to see how, even in our ancient and honourable Society, the jewel truth has become encrusted until to outward view it is like the pebble ignorance.

Finally, I would urge that the mission of Masonry is not yet ended; its practical services in preserving knowledge in days when the possession of such knowledge was too often the passport to a shameful death deserve to be ever kept in remembrance, and even now it may be that in a Lodge close tiled we can impart to each other matters of deep interest which yet it may not be well to publish for the indiscriminate use of the outer world.

The mission of masonry is search after Light ineffable—after perfect Truth.

What saith Hermes? —

As below, so above—and as above, below.

Saith Picus of Mirandula, —

Who knows himself knows all things in himself.

Saith Abipili, —

I admonish thee, whosoever thou art that desirest to dive into the inmost part of nature: if that thou seekest thou findest not within thee thou wilt never find it without thee.

Saith Pletho, —

Invoke not the self conspicuous image of nature.

Saith Synesius, —

To these he gave the ability of receiving the knowledge of light;
Those that were asleep he made fruitful from his own strength.

Time was; Time is; Time will be.

There was no beginning, there will be no end—
  Force; all pervading.
    A. U. M.

Motion perpetual and rhythmical, the time alone varying.
  Matter eternal, in forms infinite.

After excitement, birth: then repose, after calm, refructification,
  Death, concentration; Life, expansion.

Yet Death the beginning of Life and Life the forerunner of Death.

The circles infinite, boundless, from the centre-force so to infinity.
  The centre omnipresent, the circumference non-existent.

Curve and recurve from the moneron up to the essence.
  World without end.

THE FIRST DEGREE.

THE usual lecture on the first Tracing Board is so well known that I need only refer to it by name, and I do not now propose to enlarge upon the moral maxims beautiful as they are which are commonly deduced from the symbols we know so well; they are too trite, too well worn to need further re-iteration. The explanations usually given moreover, are those which lie immediately on the surface of freemasonry; and did freemasonry go no farther, were there no more interesting secrets hidden in its depths; it would indeed be a most paltry study; a valuable charitable organization, vast in extent, far reaching in its aims and power, but most empty and unsatisfying to those who have joined our body in the hope of extending their knowledge.

It is usually stated in the above named lecture, that Freemasonry is a beautiful system of morality, veiled in allegory and illustrated by symbols. This is partly true; nor is the veil to be lifted or the symbols understood without some trouble, it is however something more than this for those who have the patience to study and the wit to comprehend the mysteries which lie hid in symbols, words and ceremonies often apparently meaningless or trivial. To those for whom it is merely a system of morality we can leave the Masonry of aprons and badges, the dull changeless ritual connected with the worship of an Anthropomorphic Deity and the fanciful titles of a tinsel rank— they can never understand the nature of the mystic tie which binds those even, who have but just passed the threshold of the real temple, with the dwellers in the adytum, infinite as is the distance between the initiate and the adept.

First as to the antiquity of Masonry. While there
is no reasonable doubt that secret societies for the preservation and extension of knowledge have existed
from prehistoric times, and that much of the symbolism in our Lodges is derived from Egyptian, Chal-
daic and Babylonian sources, it is at the same time
beyond question that many of the statements in our
ritual have little further warranty than the opinions of
those who drew it up about 160 years ago when in A. D.
1717 the descendants of the Building fraternities laid
aside their purely operative character and Freemasonry
assumed somewhat of its present form.

I need not pause to consider how much weight
should be allowed to the theological opinions of brothers
who could believe that at the command of a certain
mythical Joshua the earth's movements were stopped
in order to further the marauding of an obscure tribe
of Asiatics, but will only premise that in speaking of
the *origin* of Freemasonry I refer to the times and
opinions whence our oldest ceremonies are derived.

For the origin of Freemasonry regarded in this
light, we must go back to that dim twilight of the ages
of which no written record now remains; it existed
æons before the word from which some derive its name
(the *Hebrew Massan or Massang, a stone quarry)
was formed, and was but a branch of the knowledge,
which was then so jealously guarded by its possessors.
At a very early period the necessity of imparting
knowledge to those alone who could fitly use it, in fact
of not trusting a child with edged tools, was recognized
by the master minds among men—" non cuivis homini
contingit adire Corinthum;"—and to go no farther
back than some 4000 years, from which date at any
rate certain of our ceremonies have existed (the forms
of course being modified by time), we may readily

* Higgins suggests. ' Maia sons '—among other fanciful deriva-
tions—Mackenzie—the mediæval latin Maçonner, to build; or perhaps
the old german Metzen, to cut (R. M. Cyclopædia.)

conceive that the number of men who were then capable of understanding the hidden mysteries of nature was small indeed. Law could hardly be said to exist, or at best it was the law of the strongest, and each secret therefore which patient toil and clumsy appliances had wrested from the bosom of nature, was, for the benefit of the finder and his associates, disguised in symbols and its application veiled in allegory. As a result of this habit many valuable discoveries were lost and we are even now in these later days rediscovering much which ages ago formed part of the lore of the Chaldees.

It is unnecessary to discuss the fable that the world was created from nothing in seven days ending on a Friday evening 4000 years B. C. This figment has served to satisfy the curiosity of the ignorant and vulgar for a considerable time, but in a Lodge just perfect and regular we need not so degrade The Great Architect of the Universe as to fashion him after our puny likenesses.

The theory of the constitution of this planet and its place in the solar system, was doubtless to some extent recognized from very early times; it was believed, at the earliest date from which we can take a departure, that this system is but a part of others too vast for our ken and that all go through the same endless round, travelled alike by the earth and by the bodies we now inhabit, of expansion, contraction, and re-expansion, all in strict obedience to fixed natural law.

Naturally however, the demonstration of this theory could then be comprehended by but few, and in these later days when thought and enquiry are comparatively free, I shall be pardoned, I hope for the trite remark, that the Elohistic and Jehovistic accounts of Genesis to be found in the Hebrew writings we call the Volume of Sacred Law—are simply broad allegorical statements, of doubtful authorship, poetical, and like all good poetry containing perhaps an element of truth in the kernel, if we have only wit to crack the nut.

It may also not be out of place here to state briefly what meaning the word " God " is intended to convey in the following pages.

Pari passu with the evolution of the human race there has apparently been developed an anthropomorphic tendency which has led to the conception of a man-like being of illimitable powers to whose agency is to be ascribed the existence of every thing. The names given to this being are too numerous for recapitulation here, they refer to every known vice or virtue in its highest form of development.

Masonically speaking however the only profession of belief required at the hands of a Mason is one in the omnipresent existence of a Force which we agree to designate God; whose infinite attributes we reverently investigate, seeking always to improve those faculties which alone enable us to make any progress however slow, and however infinitesmal, in comparison with the vastness of the subject, towards the Light.

At the door of the Lodge the Mason leaves all religious questions, but Masonry precludes no man from following the faith of his fathers, if it so seems good to him, or the convictions of his heart, his conscience or his reason.

In the terms I used just now, to wit Elohistic and Jehovistic as distinguishing two different theories of evolution, lies concealed an important fact. They are in truth two theories, one propounded by a writer who symbolized the creative force of nature under the name " El," the other by a follower of " Jah ":— Whether of these twain is the more ancient is by no means certain, and at any rate we need not enter into the question in this place.

" Elohim " is a modern Hebrew corruption of " Aleim " the plural of " Al " or " El " which in Chaldee is the sun, the creator, masculine—it is made feminine in the plural and under this symbol the feminine element, the preserver, was joined to it and the God became androgynous.

Jehovah—so pronounced according to the Masoretic punctuation, or more correctly Jahveh was anciently written Jod-he-vau-he or Ieue, is identical with " Iove " of the Latins and Etruscans—it is light symbolized by the letters Jod and Aleph, it is Alpha and Omega, Jah—it refers to the male power exclusively.

The two cults are frequently confounded one with another in the Hebrew traditions, but it may be broadly stated that the worship of Jahveh refers to a belief in one dominant force and that of Elohim to the deification of the separate manifestations of that force.

There is not much to be said for the morality of either, but at any rate while the latter degenerated into nature worship, devil worship and the lowest of superstitions, the former by virtue of its monotheistic basis had within it a germ of truth and with it we are principally concerned.

From the earliest days, so soon as man had evolved the power of grouping facts and drawing inferences from them, it may be supposed that he experienced a natural craving to find some explanation of the system he saw in universal operation around him. Ceaselessly he saw the sun apparently rise and set, the moon wax and wane, the stars in their courses all obedient to some unchanging law, the seasons in endless succession producing, ripening, dying and reproducing and he found himself, in obedience to natural instincts, the active agent in reproducing his own species. He must have quickly noticed the close analogy existing between all forms of life from the lowest to the highest, so far as he was capable of observing them, and with dimly awakened mind he ascribed it all to the operation of some mysterious being, invisible, infinitely powerful, eternal. Unable as yet to conceive all attributes united in one force he symbolized each manifestation under appropriate forms. But, while he, the initiated, and his fellows with intellects sharpened by use never committed the mistake of confounding the creature with the creator, it was not so with the outside world; *they* came to adore the symbol instead of the force symbolized, and quickly perceiving the power which knowledge gave and at the same time how dangerous a weapon it was to intrust to the brute force of the masses, the wise men, Magi, sons of Maia, Masons, kept their lore a profound secret from all *but* the initiated.

To keep their discoveries ever freshly in their minds they instituted mysteries or secret festivals with many precautions against the intrusion of the profane; from these, were in time developed the Eleusinian and other mysteries, of which more anon, and of these mysteries masonry formed a branch, but be it remembered, there were chapters within chapters; not even to every high priest of Isis was *all* the lore so patiently accumulated, so hardly won, revealed. Seed so precious was not to be sown in unkindly soil and many failed, many fainted by the way, more had not the requisite powers of mind to attain to eminence.

Naturally the first object which would strike the mind of primeval man with wonder, was the sun; impersonated as a male it was considered a God whose principal attribute was that of kindling life; it was the sun who engendered the blade of corn within the body of the Earth; he was the life giver, he it was who planted the point or speck or seed of life within the circle or womb of the universe, that centre which is every where, that circumference which is nowhere. With the sun's name were compounded adjectives signifying strength warmth, fruitfulness, brightness. He was Phra-on, Bra, Pra.—the chief Pharaoh. He is the most striking and important object depicted on this tracing board. The analogy between him and man's own power of reproducing his species soon became apparent and he was worshipped under the symbol of the phallus or linga; in this form he was called by some Priapus *i. e.* Phra-ab, pra-ab, pra-apis, ab meaning the father, hence in its full meaning "the Sun the father." How this worship was developed, fell into extremes of coarseness, and finally was stripped of that coarseness and clothed in symbols till the real meaning is difficult to find, we shall see later; for the present I would only name that the rude stone column or pillar which was an emblem of the sun, by degrees became symbolically ornamented until we have three orders of architecture you see on the board before you.

I may here name that the words pillar, pole, and their congeners are derived from the Sanscrit 'phal' to burst, to produce, to be fruitful, also a ploughshare, hence Phallus means he breaks through or passes into, and worship of the God under this form is usually known as Phallic Worship; it is common to all countries, all ages and exists still among our neighbours the Japanese and Hindus in nearly its pristine forms. Every temple was originally a microcosm of the universe as then understood, in imitation of which they were surrounded with pillars recording astronomical observations. The most usual number was 40, as at Stonehenge and Abury, two of which as in those Druidic circles were distinguished from the others, standing at the porch, as emblems of the male and female principles; they were in fact Jachin and Boaz; the real meaning of the former is Jah strengthens, Jah is hot with desire, and Boaz has the same phallic meaning referring to the other sex; the signification of pillars however and the astronomical knowledge they preserved belong more fitly to another place.

To the point within the circle I have already alluded, it was doubtless meant to symbolize the act of generation—the union of the phallus and the Yoni— and the mosaic pavement next calls for notice.

This was framed with no idle idea of beauty, further than that all knowledge is in a sense beautiful, but was probably connected with some practical use in the art of counting. I need scarcely say that when our mysteries were first celebrated, the Arabic numerals were unknown and the Chaldee must have required some such contrivance as the Chinese swan-pan to make them available for purposes of calculation, added to which the arts of writing and arithmetic were originally one, and one of the most valuable of the secrets of the initiated. To give an instance of the attainments of the ancient mathematicians I would name that 350 years B. C. the philosopher Callisthenes, grandson of Aristotle, who accompanied Alexander on his Asiatic expedition obtained in Babylon a series of astronomical observations ranging back through 1903 years, and Professor Draper states that the Babylonian estimate of the value of the cycle of the Saros (more than 6585 days, was within nineteen and a half minutes of the truth.

The mosaic pavement was probably an enormous abacus or counting board the squares or " chequers " of which were utilized in calculation: the word chequers still survives in our " Court of the Exchequer " the floor of which was originally in chequers also. The history of the shape of the Lodge and of the blazing star in the centre of the board belong more properly to the consideration of the lecture in the next degree, (though as regards the former I find I must here make some brief mention) so that there remains now but one important feature to notice namely the 72 triangles with their points outward or downward which surround the board, known as the indented or tesselated border.

The number 72 is a survival of an ancient myth. The Sun-god was thought to have divided the year into 12 months, with 12 signs, into each of which he passed successively; the whole year was divided into two hemispheres of six months each, light and darkness; expansion, contraction; life, death; during one of which the Genius of good or light prevailed, and during the other, the power of darkness or evil. Each month was divided into 12 parts, assigned to the attendants of the disciple, or vice-god who ruled the month and these multiplied by six for the hemisphere gave 72, a mystic number, which will further be explained hereafter; it referred to the discovery of the precession of the equinoxes about which I hope to speak when considering the lecture in the third degree.

The triangular form has been chosen by all ancient nations as a symbol of deity—the equilateral triangle being regarded as the most perfect of figures from the consideration that it could not be resolved any farther—it had also a special signification with which we are more immediately concerned viz:—

The letter Delta, a triangle standing on its base was used by the Greeks, who brought the idea from the East, to express the pudendum muliebre. Daleth in Hebrew and Delta in Greek signify the door of a house, also the outlet of a river, while the figure reversed, i. e. standing on its apex, was held to represent the overshadowing fringe and was an emblem of secrecy.*

I have still to refer briefly to the shape of the Lodge which is stated in the usual Lecture to be of an oblong square: in the length from East to West, in breadth between North and South, in depth from the surface of the earth to the centre and even as high

---

* On the front of the temple of Isis at Sais was the following description of her, in the form of a ▽ apex downwards *in Seven lines:*
I Isis am all that has
been that is or shall
be; no mortal man
hath ever
me unvei
le
d

as the heavens. Why the Brother or brethren who are responsible for our ritual should have considered these dimensions to form an oblong square I cannot imagine but at any rate the meaning given has nothing whatever to do with the matter.

The Lodge is no doubt the Ark or sacred Argha of the Hindus—this was an oblong vessel of a suggestively sexual character used by the High priests as a sacrificial chalice, in the worship of Isis, Astarte and similar deities. According to some of the most ancient theories the world was supposed to be destroyed and renewed at the end of certain periods and this process was supposed to be of immense, perhaps eternal duration. At the moment of destruction Brahme Maia was believed to be in a state of inaction or repose, and the male and female generative powers of nature were said to float or brood, in conjunction, on the surface of the viscous matter which was held to be the matrix of all things. This operation of the two powers is described by the Linga or Phallus in the shape of a mast fixed in the Yoni in the shape of a boat, navis, nave, Argha or Ark, floating in space.

Emblems in this form are countless and it may be that the position of the Senior Warden's column during the time that the Lodge is at work is among the number.

So in the centre of the Lodge, which is the Argha, the ark, the nave or ship as it would more correctly be painted, is the Sun, the Linga, giver of life; round the Lodge are the yonis the preservers of life, in their second capacity as guardians of his secrets, and how that life is best employed, how to get the utmost benefit from that priceless outcome of ages of evolution, it is to be hoped we may learn from the lore which has been handed down to us by our brethren in Freemasonry who have gone before.

In conclusion let me recapitulate the points wherein I conceive that the lecture as usually delivered is wrong:

1*st.*—Temples were originally in all probability round, or built in some shape more or less circular for purposes of recording astronomical-discoveries.

2*nd.*—The three reasons given why the Lodge stands on holy ground are inaccurate as they are drawn from the mythical history of a tribe of Asiatics of comparatively small real importance (though puffed up by bigoted priests and pseudo historians to an enormous apparent size) and the history of our symbols long antedates the appearance of this tribe on the world's stage.

3*rd.*—The esoteric signification of the Pillars is phallic or referring to the mystery of reproduction.

4*th.*—The Hebrew scriptures should not be arrogantly called *The* Volume of the Sacred law inasmuch as, for a Parsee, the Zend Avesta and for a Buddhist, the Dhammapada, are equally volumes of the sacred law—the obligations on each are equally binding, and both these two latter are well known by competent scholars to have been codified prior to the former.

5*th.*—The tesselated border refers to an astronomical calcu'ation.

6*th.*—The point within the circle had originally a more or less phallic signification.

7*th.*—While always careful to preserve the real ancient landmarks of our order I believe we should strive after further enlightenment rather than doggedly adhere to a ritual which tends to retain us in the prison of Ignorance.

THE SECOND DEGREE.

IN this degree as in others, the origin of certain symbols and ceremonies is customarily assigned to events as recorded in the Hebrew writings styled collectively The Bible and it will be well therefore here to state as concisely as possible what amount of credence is to be attached to these records viewed by the light of recent research. I may sum it up by saying, historically speaking, very little; scientifically, physically and morally, less; and as supernatural or divinely revealed, none at all—according to the conclusions arrived at by Professor Duncker, Dr. Inman and many other eminent writers.

The Jews can hardly be described as anything but a number of scattered bands of Asiatic thieves until the time when David consolidated them into a nation, and even then and at the highest point of their prosperity as a nation, they were but a small tribe having little influence on the then known world.

The tales of their grandeur and magnificence were mostly fictions invented in true oriental fashion, to flatter the pride and vanity of a weak people.

After their consolidation under David, the Jewish nation, which by the way was largely composed of foreign mercenaries, had all the brutal propensities of a band of bravos; they were proud, sensual, ignorant, superstitious and cruel. The prowess of David and of one special band of cutthroats which he kept as a body guard (The Gibborim) was magnified by their successors who prided themselves upon a descent from these worthies and despised all others.

So far as Moses and Joshua are concerned, there is good reason to believe that they are both mythical personages, and possibly both symbolical of the sun.

The story of Abraham, Isaac, Jacob and Moses and the first seven books of the Old Testament were fabricated shortly after the Grecian captivity or say about B. C. 800 to 700 at about which period the prophecies of Joel, Amos, Obadiah and Micah were first written down, together with all the tales about Egypt &c. and the extant traditions of David and his successors.

Much of the Pentateuch including the giving of the Law was framed about Josiah's time, but all early manuscripts (if any existed) were lost during the Babylonish captivity and when eventually committed to writing as spoken of above, the record so made was never public property but was altered from time to time to suit the priestly intrigue of the day.

The Old Testament as we have it, amalgamates Grecian, Phœnician, Babylonian, and Persian mythology and rites of worship into a heterogeneous mass which forms the Hebrew religion and it is to be noted that there is an almost total absence of Egyptian elements in Jewish books and nomenclature such as could hardly fail to exist had the tribe ever really been in Egypt; the whole story of the journey thither and exodus was probably a fiction of the Ephrainitic writer who compiled the account.

The origin ascribed to certain signs in this degree is therefore clearly erroneous and they are more probably in part derivable from the Egyptian attitude of adoration if indeed they have any very ancient origin at all.

The object to which our attention is according to ancient custom specially directed in this degree is a certain letter and in the established lecture commonly delivered on the Tracing board of this degree you are told that this represents the great Architect of the Universe.

In the various sections into which the usual Lecture is divided we are told that we are expected to make the liberal arts and sciences more expecially geometry, our study; various explanations of the constitution of the earth, &c. are also usually given, which we need no longer notice any more than it is in these days necessary to enter into an elaborate disproof that the sun moves round the earth. They sufficed for a time when men were content to accept the theories of ancient writers, even more ignorant than they, as divinely inspired and therefore of necessity true; and unhappily our uninitiated forefathers neglected the Masonic axiom which should be Truth at any cost and made their facts and explanations to accord with their theories. But indeed as has been said by a learned brother of our craft, all these apparent absurdities had an allegorical meaning; they do not.prove as some persons have imagined, the *falsity* of our religion; they only prove that the esoteric religion has not been thrown open to the vulgar. The esoteric religion was a masonic mystery and all that will, may learn.

As regards the aforesaid letter however. In ancient Lodges this was more probably written in the Hebrew form Jeue, Jod-he-vau-he or in Chaldee, Jod Aleph and Pe, for the Chaldeans adored the light and symbolized it by the letters Jod Aleph and Pe by which was meant the extreme terms of diffusion of matter in the seven planetary bodies. Jod answering to the sun, Aleph to the moon and Pe to Saturn. The connection between Jod and Jah is obvious and we may notice the sun rays which on our Tracing board are emblematical of the light, light intellectual. Jao, as the Linga, is also as may be noted placed in Daleth as the Yoni, knowledge, This name was symbolized only, never written; for our ancient brethren, aware of human tendencies towards anthropomorphism, enjoined that the name of God should be kept a profound secret and never uttered, lest men should attempt to define the indefinite, limit the illimitable, know the unknowable. and so the creature be worshipped in the place of the creator.

Of the two pillars Jachin and Boaz and their phallic meaning I have spoken in another place but these pillars and their congeners play such an important part in the history of ancient symbolism that I cannot refrain from again referring to them. Similar pillars appear to have been placed in front of temples of almost all generative gods of all nations in all climes and from the remotest antiquity, they seem not only to have been phallic emblems in which capacity their form as symbolizing the male power is sufficiently suggestive but under the name of Thoth or Hermes they represented the god of Boundaries to offend whom by removing land marks was a capital crime. There are still remains of two pillars in front of the ruins of the temple of Ceres at Eleusis. There were two in front of the temple of Baal erected in Judea about the year 900 B. C. In an engraving from an old gnostic gem *(vide Plates to Higgins Anacalypsis)* representing Samson carrying off the gates of Gaza, it may be seen that he is bearing two pillars. In the travels of Fa Hsien about A. D. 400, it is recorded that at Chu-sa-lo or Oude, the elder Hsü-ta built a shrine. On the eastern face he made the entrance, and on each side placed a stone pillar *(Giles's Record of the Buddistic Kingdoms, page 41)* similar pillars may be commonly seen in the present day even, before the gates of temples all over the east. In the ancient mysteries it was said that under or in the shadow of these pillars the initiate not only sought but acquired his knowledge. It is possible this referred to the vow of continence required from the Hierophants of Eleusis in entering upon their obligations, who as we learn from St. Jerome were accustomed to anoint themselves with hemlock juice to aid them in keeping their vows " Herbis etiam quibusdam emasculabantur: unde jam coire non poterant."—Students of psychology will be at no loss to perceive the connection between the repression of sexual instincts while the senses were continually being affected by phallic emblems and ceremonies and cerebral excitement. The reason why the columns should have been in pairs however is by no means satisfactorily established. As we have before stated the Hebrew names imply different sexes but the symbolism in the case of the female sex seems very obscure. The reader may have heard in the explanation commonly given that they were adorned with two chapiters each five cubits high and enriched with net work, lilywork, and pomegranates, one hundred in each row, as well as with two spherical balls, of which adornments certain fanciful explanations are usually given and I may as well name here that, (1) as regards the *net work*, (which by the way we may further notice in the upper chamber of the Lodge painted on this board) it is intended to symbolize the barred access to knowledge which is not to be forced open without difficulty. Anciently this symbol is referred to euphemistically in the Hebrew writings as a ' Grove;' it consisted of a simple pillar in the centre of a lozenge-like figure crossed with a lacing of cord tied up with 13 knots to represent the lunar months and was a symbol of Isis; universal mother yet still 'virgo intacta.' (2) *Lily work*. The exact meaning of this is involved in some obscurity, but as in numerous ancient Assyrian gems the fleur de lys or lily is to be found used as an antithesis to the yoni it may be supposed to symbolize creative force, or we might perhaps more correctly say, evolution. (3) *Pomegranate*. From the shape of this fruit and the number of seeds which it contains it was selected as a fitting emblem of the earth, the universal mother; it was united with bells in the adornment of the robes of the Jewish high priest. On Jachin and Boaz there were 100 pomegranates each with six leaves or rays at the top of the fruit *(Parkhurst);* on the high priest's robes there were 72 also each with six leaves; these two sets of numbers multiplied together give 600 and 432 respectively; the numbers of years in certain astronomical cycles of which more anon. I may further name that in Solomon's temple the pomegranate was united with lilies and probably with the lotus, the latter still in Buddhist symbolism the masculine triad.

Next as regards geometry and kindred studies; it would be presumptuous in me to dilate on the pleasures to be found in the study of the exact sciences; all those who tread such paths know well what rich rewards the pursuit of knowledge brings, it may however be of some interest to keep in mind, the painful struggles of our forefathers, by whose labours after light we in this day see less dimly, just as we may naturally hope that the names of those who now are engaged in a similar pursuit will, in the ages yet to come, be honourably remembered;—so through their works to speak to millions yet unborn and thus achieve their noblest immortality.

As regards the science of numbers; to quote from the late Mr. J. S. Mill, " the proposition that two and one are equal to three expresses merely a truth known to us by early and constant experience; an inductive truth, and such truths are the foundation of the science of number. The fundamental truths of that science all rest on the evidence of sense; they are proved by showing to our eyes and our fingers that any given number of objects, 10 balls for example, may be separation and re-arrangement exhibit to our senses all the different sets of numbers the sum of which is equal to 10."

Passing over the earliest struggles of primeval
man with numbers, the most ancient division of time,
though this too is prehistoric, was probably.

1 year	= 12 months	= 1 circle	= 12 signs
1 month	= 30 days	= 1 sign	= 50 degrees
1 day	= 60 hours	= 1 degree	= 60 hours
1 hour	= 60 minutes	= 1 hour	= 60 minutes
1 minute	= 60 seconds	= 1 minute	= 60 seconds

and when man had arrived at this point he must already
have made considerable progress in astronomy, he
must have discovered the lunar year of 13 periods
each of about 28 days, which would presumably be far
nearer the truth than the solar year as up to that time
known.

He would have further divided the circle thus,
taking the five fingers of the hand as the initial means
whereby such calculations were wrought out:—

5 degrees	= 1 dodecan	=	5 degrees
2 dodecans	= 1 decan	=	10 ,,
3 decans	= 1 signs	=	30 ,,
3 signs	= 1 quadrant	=	90 ,,
4 quadrants	= 1 circle	=	360 ,,

The cycle of 432 years to which I have before
alluded and which was the base of the great Indian
cycles was arrived at in the following manner. In
each sign there are 6 decans and 12 signs in the year
or circle; therefore 72 became a sacred number referring to the ordinary year and this again multiplied by
6 became the great year, of 432. The reader will
recollect the 72 triangles forming the tesselated border,
which I referred to in a former place, and numberless
other instances where 72 is found in ancient writings
and mysteries will doubtless be called to mind.

The cycle of the Neros, or of 600 years, arose in
all probability later, i. e. so soon as it had been discovered by astronomical observations that a precession

of the Equinoxes at the rate of about 1 degree in 72 years ($50''9'''\frac{3}{8}$ in a year) was nearly correct, or at any rate more nearly correct than the earlier calculation.

The complete elucidation of these numbers in their different bearings would take too long for our present purpose and the calculations themselves are moreover within the reach of all; suffice it to say that the numbers 5, 7, (this latter number from the number of the planets, the Sun, the Moon, Jupiter, Mercury, Mars, Venus and Saturn) 12, 60, 72, 432, and 600 have from time immemorial been held sacred and will be found intimately connected with a very large proportion of the myths in which ancient scientific discoveries were veiled. Their esoteric meaning was known to the initiated and it is almost beyond question that in the most ancient times from which our order dates, the High priests of the Light that had no written name, were themselves Arch Masons; who else indeed could have constructed the temples each of which was a microcosm of the universe so far as known and every detail of which recorded a discovery?

How the tide of knowledge ebbed and flowed just as victory inclined either to the side of brute ignorance, sensuality, and darkness, or to the side of truth and light is written in the history of every nation, and in the earliest times of which that history speaks we shall find the Brahme-Maia, Linga-Yoni, that is, the male and female principles in union, were the symbol of the deity adored.

After a while came division; in the East the followers of the Linga prevailed and the Yonijahs were driven westward; hence the wars of the Mahabharata, the fabled wars spoken of in the Greek myths, and other legends. Unhappily too not to end there, for the same contest has been waged but some few centuries ago, how cruelly let hecatombs of martys tell, in our own land between the followers of the Virgin the universal mother and the followers of the Creative power. No where has knowledge found a more bitter foe than among the ranks of the priesthood, the half-initiated, possessed of that little knowledge which is such a perilous acquisition, who seeing, have not seen, and hearing, have not understood. It is against these. that we as Masons seeking after light have often to contend, though mindful always of the benefits we owe them, for though done unwittingly, it is to them we owe the preservation of many of our mysteries.

To paraphrase a saying of that great sage Confucius :—

Man's highest knowledge is to gauge his ignorance.

IN THE THIRD DEGREE.

We now come to the tracing board of the third degree, fitly called the sublime degree of a M. M. in that we here touch the threshold of our knowledge, here complete the triune symbol of Force creative, Force preservative and Force destructive, the real trinity; so complete and interwoven that each act of either is but the operation of all.

Unlike the other Tracing boards, this one contains no symbol which is not self evident to every M. M. but it is not so generally known how the rites in which we have all taken part originated, or what they were originally intended to symbolize, and these points I will endeavour to explain as briefly as may be.

It may perhaps not be uninteresting if before going farther I give as far as I am permitted a short account of the rite of initiation as anciently practised at least as far as the paralellism to our own third degree extends. Of the higher and more perfect rites I shall hope to speak on some future occasion.

I have chosen the mysteries of Isis as an example as these have perhaps been more commented upon than others but those of Eleusis, Dionysos, of the Essenes and in the present day of certain Hindu sects might be described in almost the same words.

MYSTERIES OF ISIS.

The initiate was divested of all clothing, sprinkled with water by the priest, brought into the temple and placed in the East at the feet of the goddess where he remained in meditation for ten days, fasting from wine, flesh, fish, and all luxurious food, and preserving strict continence *

After ten days he was clothed in a new linen garment and brought into the inner apartment of the sanctuary where an oath of secrecy was exacted from him, he was then blindfolded and subjected to great torments, eventually being left, with the bandage indeed taken from his eyes, but in total darkness in the rock hewn labyrinth beneath the Temple. While he remained here his senses were appealed to by terrible sounds, flashes of lurid light, apparitions in horrible forms flitted by him, disgusting odours filled the air, until weary and worn out with fasting and excitement the neophyte believed himself on the borders of death, whence he was finally rescued, light restored to him and certain physical explanations of the symbolical ceremonies he had gone through were communicated to him.

He was then arrayed in twelve stoles (emblematical of the months) on which were embroidered the signs of the zodiac, and the first part of the initiation then concluded with a feast.

---

* This condition will be wondered at less when it is remembered that the temples of the gods were in many cases little else than public brothels as for instance:—The Jewish Temple in the time of Eli, the temples of Mylitta, Baal, Ceres and Laksmi Nayarana, with countless others—and enforced continence in the midst of such scenes as those by which he was surrounded might naturally lead to great cerebral excitement in the initiate and consequent hallucinations.

The second degree was also prefaced like the former one with a fast of ten days, but the neophyte does not appear to have been subjected to any terrifying experiences as in the case of his initiation. It should be named however that during the interval which had elapsed between his initiation and summons to enter further into the mysteries, he had been most carefully watched; his every movement, nay almost every thought spied out and unless the results of this espionage were eminently satisfactory, he received no summons and never made further progress towards the light. Few indeed were they who were admitted to the second degree and shared the orgies of Serapis. Fewer still they who made the final step which opened the door of the adytum.

In the second degree, were communicated the secrets of astronomy, the movements of the planets in relation to the sun, and the postulant was instructed in mathematics and kindred sciences. He further received a certain portion of the revenues of the temple and shared to some extent in the sacred services. He was still kept under the same strict surveillance, he was expected to fast often, to spend much of his time in meditation and introspection, when not engaged in studying the application of such formulæ as had been entrusted to him, and finally if judged worthy he was summoned to the final initiation, the result of which was said to be either Death, Madness, or Mastery over matter.

The oath of secrecy seems to have been exacted but once, the penalty attaching to the violation of it however was invariably carried out and involved the unlawful recipient of the secret as well as the discloser. Hence, if it ever has been divulged no record remains of such an act of perfidy.

The trials to which the postulant was subjected surpassed in severity all his previous experience, were of long duration, borne with complete abstinence from food whether solid or liquid and all that can be gathered from such hints as have been dropped by those who have survived the trial, is, that after the last dread moment where human endurance had been taxed to its utmost, a semi-stupor supervened and when consciousness returned—to quote a fragment of Strobeius mentioned by Dulaure,

"Une lumière miraculeuse et divine frappe les yeux; des plaines brillantes, des prés émaillés de fleurs se decouvrent de toutes parts; des hymnes et des chœurs de musique enchantent les oreilles. Les doctrines sublimes de la science sacrée y font le sujet des entretiens. Des visions saintes et respectables tiennent les sens dans l'admiration; l'initié est rendu parfait; desormais libre, il n'est plus asservi à aucune contrainte. Couronné, et triomphant, il se promène par les régions des bien heureux, et converse avec des hommes saintes et vertueux."

To return however to the explanation of the symbols.

In order to trace these it will be necessary to go back to the time when our forefathers invented the cycle of 432 years, from a consideration of which number it is evident by inspection that they had arrived at a point of astronomical knowledge which induced them to assign the period of 2160 years (5 times the above number) for the time occupied by the sun in his progress through one sign, this would give a precessional year of 25,920 years. In this progress and in the methods they employed to correct the error in their calculation lies a portion of the secret of our rites.

Asking pardon therefore for the recapitulation of facts so well known I would here name that the earth as our forefathers were well aware has three motions; that of revolution round the sun, its parent, that of revolution round its own axis and that which has been compared to the swaying motion of a top about to cease spinning—though in this simile there is one important difference.

In a top about to cease spinning the conical rotation of the axis takes place in the same direction as the rotation of the top *about* the axis *unless* the centre of gravity of the whole mass be depressed below the point of suspension, in which case as in the case of the earth, the pole of the axis will revolve about the pole of the ecliptic in an *opposite direction* to that in which it revolves about its own axis.

This motion waxes and wanes, to and from a position of perfect parallelism to its own axis and the time occupied in so moving determines the precession of the equinoxes.

If the constitution of the earth were such that the resultant of the attractions exerted on all its parts by any other body should always pass through a definite point in its mass, its diurnal rotation would not be affected by the attraction of any other bodies. If originally revolving about a principal axis of inertia it would continue to do so and the direction of the axis would be constant. As a fact however, the attractions of various bodies, the sun and moon especially, on the oblate portion at the equator, tend to give it a rotation about an axis *in* the plane of the equator and the combination of these two rotations gives rise to a shifting of the instantaneous axis of rotation in the earth and also in space. In fact the precession of the equinoxes is a slow retrograde motion of the equinoctial points from E to W or contrary to the order of the signs *i. e.* from Aries to Pisces, and it is in consequence of this that the constellations have changed the position assigned to them by ancient astronomers.

The equinoctial points during the time of Aristarchus (300 B. C.) were fixed on the first stars of Aries and Libra, but now the first star of Aries is in that portion of the ecliptic or great circle in which the sun appears to move, which is known as Taurus, the stars of Taurus in Gemini and so on.

The stars therefore which in Aristarchus' time were in conjunction with the sun when it was in the equinox are now a whole sign or 30° to the eastward. The ecliptic is divided into 4 quadrants or arcs of 90° each, by the equinoctial points and solstices, (the latter being the periods when the sun is at its greatest distance from the equator viz: at 22nd June and 22nd December.) These quadrants are divided each into 3 arcs of 30° each, called the signs of the Zodiac and the latter are named from the constellations which happened to be found in each when the division of the ecliptic was first made. These divisions do not now coincide with the constellations owing to the retrograde movement spoken of, though the names are still preserved.

Astronomical calculations are made from that point of intersection of the equator and ecliptic which is the position of the sun in the heavens on the 21st March and which is known as the first point of Aries.

The time occupied between the periods when the earth is parallel to its own axis i. e. the time occupied in the precession of the equinoxes, the great year, is computed at 25,868 years. Our forefathers therefore found by observation that their calculations were out by a little more than a day an a quarter in each year.

They took their departure as regards time from the beginning of the precessional year when by computing backwards they found that the sun entered the first point of Aries about the 21st of our March. This day they considered the aniversary of the birth of the Sun, the creator, the life giver, to accomplish which birth it was necessary that he should have first died; they fixed the date of his death as after the 22nd or 25th of December or in the time of the winter solstice and figuratively spoke of the intercalary time as of a period when the sun wandered in Sheol the land of shadows, Hell, as early christian divines have rendered it. About the 23rd March at the vernal equinox when all nature rejoices with returning spring they celebrated the birth with annual rejoicing in allegorical ceremonies.

To these two festivals we owe the myths of the births, deaths, descents into Sheol and resurrections of all the Saviours of mankind. Osiris, Ormuzd, Mithra, Adonis, Brahma, Cristna, Hercules, Buddha, Christ, of every one of whom the same story has been told with but the trifling variations in detail induced by the difference of locality.

To show you more plainly the parallelism between the rites in which we have all participated and those of early Magi or Masons, let me briefly describe one scene the details of which have been transmitted to us by an eyewitness after a lapse of nearly two thousand five hundred years.

The scene is laid in Baalbec. The time, midnight on the 24th December some 450 years B. C.

Far above the mighty city of Heliopolis low crouching at its feet towered the temple of Baal, Lord of the sun. All through the starlit night there had been scarcely a break in the long line of worshippers thronging towards the grandest fane the world has ever seen, its origin lost in the mists of ages; which even now, in ruins mocks the greatest efforts of the mason of to-day—but then, in all its glory of hewn stone and carven pillar, of inlaid work and mystic emblem, was the seat of all the learning of the east, the repository of the lore of the Chaldees.

In the peristyle of the temple were 54 columns. The outer court was about 300 feet in length by 160 feet in breadth and covered four acres of ground, leading at the northern end into an octagonal court 160 feet in diameter. On the west, was the especial temple of Ra; on the east the smaller temple of Isis, this latter larger than the Parthenon of later days. Beneath the whole were subterranean chambers of vast extent wherein were celebrated the more hidden mysteries and wherein were held the highest chapters of the perfect arch-masons, high priests of Isis, Magi; around the great court ran double rows of pillars, in number recording the astronomical discoveries of the time. These were surmounted by a frieze on which were graven mystic signs referring also to the secrets of the initiated. The centre of the court was open to the vault of heaven.

Through the long day, thousands of priests had chanted
hymns in praise of Ra, standing in the octagonal temple wherein
was the altar of Isis, behind the altar a veil covering the
Universal Mother; on her right the figure of Osiris, on her left
the image of Typhon; the Mystic Trinity; Life, Preservation,
Death; now however no priests stood within the inner temple
and all the crowd in the outer court were hushed in silent
expectation.

Then from the aisles on either side stole files of white
robed priests and from behind the altar came the high priest of
Isis crying aloud *Hear O ye People!* this night we mourn the
death of our God Osiris. He, returning hither over the wine-
dark sea after that he had rescued the nations from darkness and
the plagues sent by the angry Gods, after that he had taught
them wisdom and given them light; was slain by Typhon dweller
in darkness, jealous of the blessings given to mortals. His body,
rent asunder, was scattered to the four winds, neither was the
place of burial known. Him, sorrowing, Isis long sought;
reverently she collected the members save only those devoured
by the fish, and brought them hither. Far and wide her
lamentations resounded to the blue vault of Heaven, nor was
Ra unmindful of her prayers. Again he raised the dead to life
and light returned to bless the dwellers on the earth.

Then brought the acolytes the sacred ark and placed it before
the high priest. In front of it came and stood a youth as
beautiful as the day. Him the high priest smote till as one
lifeless he fell into the ark, its door was closed upon his form,
and then the high priest rent his clothes and cried with a loud
voice, Osiris our God is dead. Lights were put out and from
all the people rose a great wail, as of a mother mourning for
her first-born.

All through the night, through the next day and till the
morning of the third day, feigned the priests to search for. the
limbs of the youth that had been slain. Then when the morning
broke and all the people waited as before in the great court of
the temple, came the high priest and raised the youth from out
the ark saying.

Rejoice O Sacred Initiated your God is risen, his death, his
pains and sufferings have worked your salvation. And all the
people shouted and sang praises to Osiris celebrating his new
birth with great festivity.

The connection of this myth with our mysteries is
so obvious that I need say little more in explanation of
the tracing board of this degree, but it may not unnatu-
rally be demanded from those who show that the Hebrew
Scriptures are no more divine than the Vedas, the

Avesta, the Dhammapada or the Koran and that the
Mosaic cosmogony is but the unscientific speculation of
some literary Jew who lived about 800 or 900 years
B. C.—that some better theory shall be supplied to fill
the place of that which has been demonstrated to be false.

Such a task has been happily accomplished.
Known or guessed at by the Magi of old, lo-t, when the
tide of knowledge ebbed for nearly 1200 years, per-
ceived by Kant, worked out by Laplace in 1796 and
now when we may fondly hope we are being carried by
a flood tide to a higher point than heretofore known,
triumphantly established, we can assuredly boast of a
probable theory of the genesis of the world.

I will endeavour to place an outline of this hypothesis before you in the briefest terms I can command
in order that I may the better show how far the fragments
of ancient writings which are left to us, bear out the
opinion above expressed as to the knowledge possessed
by the sages of old.

At a very early date (time disappears in dealing
with such periods as those of which I now speak) the
entire solar system consisted of the sun, a mass of infinitely
attenuated vapour in a state of incandescence, extending
at least so far as would include the orbit of Neptune;
the mean distance of which planet from the sun is about
2856 millions of miles.

Whether such a mass would cool quicker at the
surface by radiation or at the centre by pressure we have
not sufficient data to show, but at any rate its contraction
would induce currents of motion the movements of which
would be determined by local influences but which would
finally end in a definite rotation in one direction and the
mechanical consequences of which would be that the
mass must at last assume the form peculiar to rotating
bodies the particles of which move freely upon each
other, viz:—an oblate spheroid, flattened at the poles
and bulging at the equator because at the equator the
centrifugal tendency generated by rotation is greatest.

Furthermore, as the mass contracts, its velocity must increase (the total quantity of rotation being unalterable) and so its poles would become more and more flattened, its equatorial zone protrude still more until, the centrifugal tendency at the equator, being greater than the force of gravity there, this zone, unable to keep pace with the rest of the mass in its contraction would at last be left behind as a detached ring girdling at an ever increasing distance the central mass.

Such a ring, unless subjected to absolutely equal forces in every direction must at last break up into fragments; with each fragment the same transition to oblate speroidal forms would take place, they would coalesce into globes and by the greater power of attraction they would assume as consolidated bodies would revolve round the sun and from mechanical considerations would also revolve on their own axes. They in their turn behaving in like manner would abandon similar rings hereafter to form similar satellites.

These smaller bodies would of course cool first until their temperature permitted the manifestation of vegetable and animal life and one of those smaller bodies is the planet we inhabit.

If this hypothesis be true, we can scarce overrate its importance, and as to its truth let me quote the dictum of one of the master minds among men, the late Mr. J. S. Mill.

"There is in this theory no unknown substance introduced on supposition nor any unknown property or law ascribed to a known substance, it is an example of legitimate reasoning from a present effect to a possible past cause according to the known laws of that cause." *(System of Logic B. III Ch. XIV.)*

And now to give a few examples of the lore of the Chaldees, which the curious may find collected and translated in that valuable work, ' *Ancient Fragments* ' *by J. P. Cory.*

" We learn that matter pervades the whole world, as the Gods also assert."

" He makes the whole world of fire, and water, and earth, and all nourishing ether."

" Suspending their disorder in well disposed zones."

" Oh all ruling Sun, Spirit of the world, Power of the world, Light of the world."

" All things, therefore, are three, but not one; Hyparxis, Power, and energy."—

I might add many more, but the above are probably sufficient for my present purpose which is to show that the greater part of our rites and symbols refer to ancient discoveries in physical science. In fact to quote from Mr. S. Baring Gould.

" The priests of ancient times were also philosophers, but not being able always to preserve their intellectual superiority, their doctrines became void of meaning, hieroglyphs of which they had lost the key, and then speculation ate its way out of religion, and left it an empty shell of ritual observance void of vital principle." *(Origin and development of Religious Belief. P. 120.)*

Here, with a theory of the origin of life I bring this brief essay on the Degree of Death to a close, and fitly so, for Life and Death are so subtilely interwoven that each is but the genesis of the other, the terms are interchangeable.

Whether when the tide of life has ebbed to the slack and loosed the thread that binds each atom to its neighbour, ultimate molecules can re-unite and leave no important break in the continuity of consciousness, we may reasonably doubt, but this we know, that matter is eternal.

We live in deeds, not years; in thoughts, not breaths;
In feelings, not in figures on a dial.
We should count time by heart throbs. He most lives
Who thinks most, feels the noblest, acts the best.
(Bailey's *Festus.*)

This is Life—the Ignorance that dares not face a truth it fears to know is Death indeed.

DELTA.

www.ingramcontent.com/pod-product-compliance
Lightning Source LLC
Chambersburg PA
CBHW061238260626
47172CB00003B/910